Up Along
Down Along
Under and Over

Diane Wilmer
Pictures by
Iris Schweitzer

Collins

William Collins Sons & Co Ltd
London · Glasgow · Sydney · Auckland
Toronto · Johannesburg

For Clive
who showed me the way

Reading consultant: Mia Beaumont

First published 1985
© text Diane Wilmer 1985
© illustrations Iris Schweitzer 1985

ISBN 0 00 171229 2 (hardback)
ISBN 0 00 171262 4 (paperback)

Printed in Great Britain by
William Collins Sons & Co Ltd., Glasgow

Sam and Jan were good pals.
They lived in the same street,
went to the same school and
were both the same age, but
sometimes they got fed up
with each other.

"I'm going to play with a big boy, not a baby," said Jan to Sam and went to find Harry.

"We'll go to the park," said Harry.

"I'm coming too," said Sam.
"OK," said Harry.
The park was big and wide,
with lots of roundabouts.

Harry played good games.

"Can you cross the park without putting your feet on the ground?" he asked.

"NO!" said Jan and Sam.

"You can, you know," said Harry.

"If you go UP ALONG DOWN ALONG UNDER AND OVER."

"Up a down under . . .?" said Sam.
"No!" said Harry. "UP ALONG
DOWN ALONG UNDER AND OVER."
"What's that?" asked Jan.
"It's a way you can go across the park,"
said Harry, and he drew a picture
in the sand for them.

"If you can cross from here to that ice-cream van over there without putting your feet on the ground . . . I'll buy you an ice lolly," said Harry.

Jan and Sam looked at the ice-cream van.
"It's a long way," said Sam.
"What if we *have* to touch the ground?"
asked Jan.

9

Harry looked at Sam and Jan,
they weren't really very big.
"All right," he said. "I'll let you touch
the ground if you have to but you must
say SNIBS, or you'll be out."
"SNIBS!" said Jan and Sam.
"Yes, now off you go," said Harry.
"And *no cheating!*"

'What goes UP?" asked Jan.
They looked around.
'I think the climbing frame
goes UP," said Sam.

It did . . .
so they went UP!
It was fun up there.
Up in the world.
Up on top.
Right UP!

"ALONG is next," said Jan.
"Up along . . .? The bar!" yelled Sam.
So along they went . . .

"Come along, come along,
come along with me.
Come along the bar and
we'll see what we can see,"
said Jan.

"I can see DOWN,"
said Sam.
"UP ALONG DOWN!"
said Jan and zoomed
down the pole.
"*Wheeeee!*"

Down below.
Down to land.
Down to earth.
Down to the ground.

"Ooh!" shouted Jan.
"I've touched the ground!"

"Say SNIBS – or you'll
be out!" yelled Sam.
"SNIBS! SNIBS! SNIBS!"
shouted Jan, jumping
up and down.
"Get off the ground,"
said Sam.

Jan looked around,
and jumped onto the first thing
she saw . . .
. . . A big concrete block.
"What next?" she asked.
"I've forgotten," said Sam.
"Oh no," said Jan. "So have I.
Let's start from the beginning.
UP ALONG DOWN ALONG
UNDER AND OVER."

"Up the frame . . . along the bar . . .
down the pole . . . And now?"
"ALONG," said Sam.
"That's right," said Jan.
"UP ALONG DOWN ALONG. Come on."

Bong along.
Bong along.
Bong along . . . STOP!
"We've finished along,"
said Jan.

"UNDER now," said Jan.
"Under what?" asked Sam.
"Under the . . . ."

. . . "HORSE!"

Get right under – on the ground.
Get right under – underneath.
Get right under, under, under.
Wriggling UNDER AND OUT!

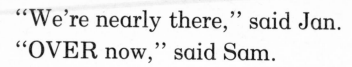

"We're nearly there," said Jan.
"OVER now," said Sam.
"Over there," said Jan.

"Over *where?*" asked Sam.
"The bridge," said Jan.
"How?" said Sam. "We can't
walk to the bridge."
"I know," said Jan. "But
we can roll. Come on."

"I'm coming," said Sam.

"I'm there," said Jan.
"Catch me if you can,"
shouted Sam.

"UP ALONG DOWN ALONG
UNDER AND OVER," said Jan and Sam,
and ran . . . over the bridge.

Over and over
over and done,
over and over
OVER AND OUT!

Harry was waiting for them by
the ice-cream van.
"Hurray! You've done it," he said.
"Here are your ice lollies."
"Let's do it again," said Sam.
"YES! Let's do UP ALONG DOWN
ALONG UNDER AND OVER over and
over and over again," said Jan.

And they did.